Hope on a

An African creation myth

retold by **Geraldine McCaughrean**

On loan from

**SCHOOL
LIBRARIES
RESOURCES
SERVICE**

Telephone 020 8200 8948
Fax   020 8201 3018
E-mail   slrs@barnet.gov.uk

BARNET
LONDON BOROUGH

New contact details:
School Libraries
Resources Service
Phone 020 8359 3931
Fax 020 8201 3018
slrs@barnet.gov.uk

LONDON BOROUGH OF BARNET
CANNOT LIBRARIES

16 JUL 2001

MOR.

30131 03639333 5

LONDON BOROUGH OF BARNET

Withdrawn

At the beginning, on the very first day, Creator-man made Sun and Moon and perched them on a bough of Heaven. There they sat, like two monkeys on the same branch. They were brothers, and Creator-man had given them each a fine yellow buckskin coat, with fringes of golden ribbon.

But of course they were no sooner left alone than they quarrelled – brothers do, don't they? Moon gave his brother a shove and toppled him off the perch. He fell, like a big orange melon – splat in the mud.

Up jumped Sun, wiped himself clean, and scrambled up aloft again. Ooooh, he was sizzling angry, spitting mad. He took Moon by an arm and a leg, and slung him down, ripping the yellow fringes off his jacket, bruising his yellow face and covering him from head to foot in mud.

"Stop it this instant!" shouted Creator-man, when he saw them brawling. "If you can't be friends, you must live at different ends of Heaven!"

And so they did. From then on, Sun shone during the day, and Moon shone at night – except that his shine was all sullied with mud, and his grubby face would not come clean either. (That's why night is so much darker than day.)

Creator-man went on making the world. He made clouds, and the cockerel lightning who cackles from cloud to cloud. He made stars and rain and the rainbow which stops the rain. He made the two kinds of air, warm and cold, the one full of grass seed, the other seeded with hail.

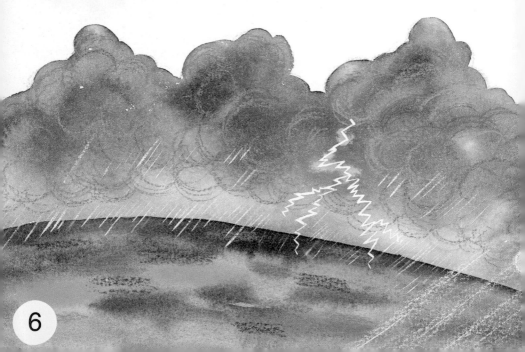

Brother Sun gave him the light to work by, but no warmth. Sun kept that to himself, rolling up his ribbony rays and storing them in a big earthenware pot. It never occurred to him that the world needed their life-giving warmth.

Creator-man made First Man and First Woman, and set them down on the Earth. In six days the world was finished, but it did not please him as much as he had hoped. The grass did not grow lush. And the cows which ate it did not grow fat. Nor did First Man and Woman.

In their little hut, they raised lots of sons and daughters – the bravest children you ever saw – but life on the Earth was no Paradise. Without the Sun's warmth, the grass was yellow, the cows thin, and the people shivering cold.

And there were monsters, too.

Creator-man did not make the monsters: they must have been there already. First Man and First Woman could hear them at night, howling and trumpeting or flapping by on great leathery wings.

First Man raised the hut up on stilts, to keep the monsters out. But he could not fetch the cows inside, to keep them safe. Cows cannot climb ladders.

So his brave children went out, with spears and sticks, and fought the monsters – trapped them in tar pits, drowned them in lakes, and left their giant bones and sabre teeth littering the countryside.

13

At last it was safe to build huts on the ground, instead of on stilts, and at last the cows were safe to graze, even though they were still thin and hungry and gave watery milk.

Creator-man was very pleased to see how brave they were, those children of First Man and First Woman. "If they dare this, what will they not dare?" he asked himself. "Perhaps they can make a Paradise for themselves after all. Now let me see. Who is the bravest of them all?"

As more and more people were born, and built their huts here and there across the Earth, boys from one village married girls from another and celebrated with a feast.

But such feasting cost the parents of the bride dear, for it meant killing and roasting a cow.

And there were so few cows!

Abala's father, for instance, had only one scrawny animal to give his family milk.

Even so, he would gladly have spared it to see his darling daughter happily married. She was as beautiful as the star-powdered sky, as slender as a willow, as strong as rope. The sound of her singing, as she fed the skinny chickens, made the deer swivel their ears, the ants stir in the earth.

But Abala refused to marry.

19

Every boy in her village wanted to marry her. Boys in every other village wanted to marry her. But Abala would have none of them. "I am waiting for the right man," she said. "I shall know when I see him."

One chilly noon, while Abala milked her father's cow, a rope came snaking down out of Heaven – CRACK!– like a whip. It startled the cow so much that she trotted off.

Some girls might have trotted away as well, but not Abala. She walked round the rope and fingered its fraying end. Then she took hold with both hands and it lifted her off the ground.

Up she went, past the balding treetops, past the stringy clouds, past birds fluffed up against the cold. At last she reached a round-hut, rather like her own but seventy times as big.

23

An old lady greeted her and helped her climb indoors. "I am sorry to disturb your milking, my dear," she said, "But my son was passing your house recently and saw you feeding the chickens. He has a great fancy to marry you."

"Has he indeed!" said Abala. "Well, who exactly is your son?"

"Why the Sun, of course, child!" replied the old lady.

It was rather startling for the girl – one moment to be milking a cow, the next to be standing in the house of the Sun.

But Abala simply leaned her head to one side and said, "I shall hear what your son has to say."

Just then, Sun came home and took Abala walking in the gardens of Heaven. Looking around, she saw big-petalled flowers, the colour of sunset, fountains of glittering rainwater, arbours of birds, filled with birdsong, and herds of chestnut cows – fat and glossy and full of milk.

While Abala admired his home, the Sun was admiring Abala. Her beauty entranced him. "If you will marry me, I'll give you a fine big wedding present!" he promised, and showed her a huge earthenware pot which stood in the corner of the hut.

When she peeped inside, Abala saw that the pot contained the Sun's rays, all coiled up like ribbons and runners of carpet. They were so bright that her eyes were dazzled, so hot that the pot was painful to touch.

"I shall marry you, my lord Sun,"
said Abala, "For I see now that you
are the husband I have been waiting
for. I think we shall be very happy."

So they were married. Abala and the Sun had three sons in the first three years of their marriage, and Abala spent her days playing with them in the gardens or milking the numberless cows of Heaven.

Then one night, as she and her husband lay beneath a bedspread of cloud, she said, "Let me go and visit my family. It is three years and more since I've seen them, and I left with no time to say goodbye. Please let me go."

Grudgingly the Sun agreed. "As long as you come back soon," he said. Abala's mother-in-law lowered her down on the same length of rope – to the very edge of Abala's village. (It gave her father's cow a great shock.)

When her father and mother saw her standing there, shivering in the chilly sunlight, they burst into tears of joy. "Oh, can it really be you? We thought, when you disappeared, that wild animals had eaten you! Where have you been, child?"

So Abala explained about the rope and the Sun and the wedding and her three fine sons.

When she finished, her father was dancing about out of sheer joy. "Kill the cow and roast it!" he crowed. "We'll feast and dance and sing tonight, because our beautiful daughter is not dead – because she is married! Even though she is a grand lady now, living in Heaven with a lordly husband, she remembered her old parents and came home to visit them! Kill the cow and roast it, I say!"

"But Father, you have only the one cow!" said Abala anxiously. "What will become of you if you kill it in honour of me?"

"Let come what comes," said her father waving his hands in the air and tossing his head as he danced. "It is the custom, and the custom must be kept. My daughter is married and has three fine sons, and still in her happiness she did not forget us!"

The whole village was happy to hear the good news, happier still to join in the feast.

37

But Abala, as she sat in the place of honour and ate roast beef to the sound of drums and whistles, could not help comparing Earth with her home in Heaven. Down here the land was so dismal and comfortless and cold.

At the end of the week, she kissed her parents goodbye, walked to the edge of the village and once again found the rope hanging down from the sky.

Her family waved until she was out of sight. Then they turned sadly homewards, wondering how they would live without even one scrawny cow to give them milk.

As soon as Abala reached home, she went to the corner of the big hut and found the earthenware jar. Dragging it to the doorway, she lifted off the lid and, with a mighty P-U-S-H, tipped it over, so that the contents spilled out.

Like the ribbons from a sewing-basket, like carpets from a merchant's overturned cart, the Sun's golden rays unfurled out of Heaven, fluttering a little on the breeze.

When the pot was empty, Abala
took a stick and went outdoors.
She flicked the rumps of thirty
fat, chestnut cows and
stampeded them through
the hole in the clouds.

They fell with the lightness
of rain – a shower of cows –
and when they touched the
ground, sat down until
they got over the shock.

Villagers ran out to stare at the fat, gleaming beasts sitting in their gardens and in their fields. The cows stared back with large, brown eyes. Then suddenly both cows and villagers began to feel warm sunlight falling on their backs.

The yellow pasture started to turn green; the trees came into blossom. Flies droned through the hot air, and the grain ripened at the tips of the long grass.

"Even in Heaven our daughter thinks of us!" said Abala's father, beaming almost as brightly as the Sun's rays.

At first, the Sun himself was annoyed with Abala for giving away the precious contents of the earthenware pot. But she stroked the sleeve of his yellow buckskin coat and said gently, "Weren't they my wedding present? Weren't they mine to do with as I saw fit?"

Then the Sun looked down at the Earth and saw how it was changing in the warmth. He saw people look up at Heaven with smiling faces and call out blessings on Abala and her lordly husband.

And he decided not to reef in the yellow ribbons and runners of sunshine.

"I was very kind to share my wealth with the poor little people down below, wasn't I?" he would say from time to time, and Abala would reply, "Yes, my dear, very kind." Then she would catch the eye of her mother-in-law and wink and smile and go on milking the numberless cows of Heaven.